MIRACLE
AT THE PLATE

The #1 Sports Series for Kids

MIRACLE AT THE PLATE

LITTLE, BROWN AND COMPANY

New York ❧ An AOL Time Warner Company

First Paperback Edition

Matt Christopher® is a registered trademark
of Catherine M. Christopher.

ISBN 0-316-13926-2 (pb)

Library of Congress Control Number 67-10220

25   24   23   22   21   20   19

COM-MO

Printed in the United States of America

To
Pam, Chuck, and Chris

MIRACLE
AT THE PLATE

1

Skeeter walked to the plate for the first time against the Barracudas and the men in the outfield stepped back. There were two outs. Joey Spry was on first, and it was the top of the first inning.

Last year the first time Skeeter faced a pitcher was in a scrub game. He had hit a home run over the left-field fence and had run around the bases twice. He had to run around twice because the first time didn't count. He had run the wrong way.

This year Skeeter hadn't seemed to have learned much more about baseball. Yet, so far, he led the Grasshopper Baseball League in batting. In three games he had been to bat seven times and had collected five hits for an average of .714.

"Come on, Skeet! Drive it!" someone on the bench yelled. Others joined in the cry.

Skeeter heard the guys chuckling behind him. They thought it was funny that he batted cross-handed. He was a right-handed hitter, but he gripped the bat with his left hand above his right, just the opposite from the way ordinary right-hand hitters gripped theirs.

He didn't stand erect at the plate either, but crouched forward with his legs far apart. He was tall and thin and clumsy. He knew he was clumsy, but he couldn't help it. When he was in a hurry his legs seemed to get in the way and he'd stumble all over the place before he'd get where he wanted to.

Mom said he was growing too fast, and not to worry about it. So he didn't.

He took a called strike that cut the outside corner, then two balls. The next was belt-high. He laid his bat into it.

The blow was solid. The ball sailed out to left center field. Joey Spry ran all around to home and Skeeter stopped on second for a clean double.

The crowd yelled and applauded. The Milky Way fans shook their heads unbelievingly and laughed.

First baseman Bogy Adams was up next. He fouled off two pitches, then socked a high fly to short center. The center fielder ran in and made a one-handed catch. Three outs.

The Milky Ways ran out to the field. All except Shadow McFitters, who ambled out to the mound as if he had all day. Shadow was a southpaw, tall and even skinnier than Skeeter, who was his pal.

Shadow hardly had any speed at all. Nor did he have much of a hook. But he did have good control. He whiffed the first two guys and the next grounded out to short for a quick half inning.

The Milky Ways threatened to score during their turn at bat, but didn't succeed. The Barracudas came up again. Their first hitter blasted the first pitch out to left field. It was going deep.

Out in left field Skeeter Miracle turned and ran. His feet tangled and he stumbled. Somehow he kept from falling. By the time he was erect again the ball was sailing over his head. He reached for it and was shy by only inches. The ball struck the ground and bounced out to the fence.

Skeeter hustled after it, picked it up, and

pegged it to the shortstop, Tip Miles. The hitter reached third for a triple.

Skeeter socked his bare fist into his glove disgustedly and kicked the grass. He should have had that fly, he thought. If he hadn't stumbled he would have.

A single drove in the run. Before the half inning was over the Barracudas put across two more to go ahead of the Milky Ways, 3 to 1.

In the top of the third Skeeter knocked out a single, but the Milky Ways couldn't score. The Barracudas put across another run, and that was Skeeter's fault, too. He had charged in after a fly ball, tried to make a shoestring catch, and missed it. The ball bounced out to the fence, and the hitter got three bases.

Skeeter was sure that Coach Jess O'Hara was going to replace him then and there, because the coach turned and shook his head. But Skeeter stayed in.

Roger Hyde, playing center field, didn't like it one bit either. Matter of fact, if it were up to Roger, Skeeter wouldn't play at all. He'd have Tommy Scott play, just because Tommy was his next-door neighbor and his best pal. As a ball player, though, Tommy wasn't anything to boast about, in Skeeter's opinion.

When the Barracudas were finally retired, Skeeter trotted in from the outfield, his glove folded in his hand.

"What are you trying to do, Miracle?" snorted Roger. "Be a hero?"

Skeeter flushed. "I was sure I could catch that ball, if that's what you're talking about," he said.

"Well, you saw what happened. You should've waited for the bounce."

"I know that now," Skeeter grunted.

Third baseman Henry Mall led off. He swung hard at a low pitch and hit a slow grounder down to third. The Barracudas' third baseman charged in. In his haste he fumbled the ball and Henry made first.

Leo Sweetman, the stocky catcher, popped up to the pitcher, and Shadow struck out. Then Tip Miles and Joey Spry banged out singles, scoring Henry. Roger Hyde, the second-best hitter on the team, flied out, ending the inning.

Skeeter was surprised when he saw Jimmy Sutton going out to center in place of Roger. He was sure that he would be replaced, too. But he wasn't.

Shadow got into immediate trouble. He walked the first two men up. Something had happened to his control. He simply could not get the ball across the plate. He looked hurt when Coach O'Hara called time and sent Nick Strope in to pitch. Nick, a right-hander, struck out the first man and the second hit into a double play.

Skeeter led off in the top of the fifth. He swung at the first pitch and *smack!* A solid blow! He saw the ball reach for the sky as it sailed for deep center field. He dropped his bat and started his hurricane run around the bases. Between first and second he stumbled and almost fell. He regained his balance and kept going.

The ball soared over the center fielder's head and struck the fence. The coach at third was swinging his arm like a windmill, urging Skeeter in to home.

Skeeter headed for home, running that funny way of his.

"Slide, Skeeter!" Bogy Adams yelled. "Slide!"

Skeeter saw the catcher crouched, waiting for the throw-in. At that instant, panic swept through him.

He was afraid to slide. He didn't know how. He was going to run all the way.

2

There were only a few feet left to go. The ball was almost to the Barracudas' catcher. Skeeter watched his bare hand and mitt. He saw the ball strike the mitt just as he crossed the plate, touching it on the inside edge with his right foot.

The catcher lunged at him with the ball, but it was too late.

"Safe!" yelled the umpire.

"What?" screamed a Barracuda fan.

"Robber!" yelled another.

Skeeter slowed down as he approached

the dugout. He took off his helmet and dropped it on the ground.

"Nice going, Skeet!" cried Shadow, patting him on the back. "A real blast!"

"A beautiful hit, Skeeter," Coach O'Hara said, grinning at him. "But you should've slid. You almost didn't make it."

"He's afraid to slide, that's why," Roger Hyde said.

"Didn't think I had to," Skeeter said defensively, and sat in a vacant spot near the end of the dugout. The farther he sat from Roger, the better.

Bogy knocked a hard grounder through the pitcher's mound which almost capsized Pete Allison, the Barracudas' hurler. Spider laid down a bunt inside the third-base line. Pete Allison fielded it and threw Spider out at first by a close margin — so close that the Milky Way fans began shouting at the base umpire.

"You call that out? Oh, man!"

"Are those Barracuda guys paying you, ump?"

Other remarks were blasted at the base umpire, who was just an ordinary parent with no umpire's uniform on, only a baseball cap. Skeeter didn't like it. What was the matter with those people, anyway? Why did they yell at the umpire like that? He was as fair as he could be. They should know that.

Coach O'Hara sent Luther Lee in to bat for Henry Mall. Luther was on the fat side and would have to travel fast to reach first if he managed to hit a ball through the infield.

He blistered the first pitch over second base and made it to first in plenty of time, but that was because the throw-in was to second and from second to home in an attempt to get Bogy. Bogy scored, but Luther didn't take any chances. He stayed on first.

Leo Sweetman got to first on an error and Luther waddled to second. A throw to get Luther was wild, so Luther continued to third. The throw-in from the Barracudas' outfielder was also wild and the coach waved Luther in. Luther scored standing up and received an ovation almost as loud as Skeeter's had been.

He was sweating and breathing hard as he walked to the dugout, a big smile on his pumpkin-round face.

"You ol' speedster!" Joey Spry said, slapping Luther on the knee. "You can really move!"

"Like a bullet!" Skeeter added, laughing.

Nick and Tip both flied out to end the inning. The Milky Ways had scored three runs, putting them in front 5 to 4. Tommy Scott replaced Skeeter in left field and hauled in two high flies to help keep the

Barracudas from scoring. He struck out at the plate, at which Shadow gave Skeeter a nudge with his elbow.

"He can catch a fly," Shadow said softly, "but he can't hit worth beans."

The game ended with the score remaining 5 to 4.

Skeeter picked up his glove and walked off the field with Shadow. Presently an arm encircled him and a strong, cheerful voice boomed, "Nice game, Skeeter! Three for three! And a homer to boot! What an eye you must have!"

It was Bob, his brother, a freshman next year in college.

Shadow chuckled. "Not one, but two real good ones," he added.

Then Mom and Dad came along. They always came to see Skeeter play, even though neither of them understood much about baseball. Dad didn't care for sports, except fishing and hunting. Mom liked to sew. Half of Skeeter's, Bob's, and Dad's shirts were sewn by her own hands. And she sewed without the use of eyeglasses. Skeeter figured that he owed his good eyesight to his mother.

Thinking about Dad's hunting reminded Skeeter of the letter they had received from Aunt Arlene and Uncle Don in Spring City, Idaho. "Remember your promise that you were coming out this summer during Josh's two week's vacation," Aunt Arlene had written. "Let us know when that is so that Don can make arrangements to take his vacation at the same time . . ."

So Mom and Dad had talked it over and decided they'd go. In a way Skeeter could hardly wait to see them and his cousins again. Except that he'd have to leave Gus . . .

Mom, Dad, and Bob rode home in Dad's car, Skeeter and Shadow on their bikes. The boys talked about the game, the number of hits the Milky Ways had gotten and the number of strike-outs Shadow had. Neither of them saw the dog, a Mexican Chihuahua, come rushing out from between the bushes.

It started barking as it reached the sidewalk, a loud *woof! woof! woof!* It was hard to imagine that such a small animal could make such a loud noise.

But it had begun barking too late. Skeeter didn't see it in time. He swerved the front wheel to prevent hitting the tiny dog. The wheel struck the animal and rolled over one of its hind legs. The dog yelped and then lay there, whimpering in pain.

Horror swept through Skeeter. He jumped off the bike, ran back and knelt beside the injured animal. Shadow knelt beside him.

"That's Pancho, Tommy Scott's dog," Shadow said. "Boy, will he be upset!"

3

Skeeter realized that they were right in front of Tommy Scott's house. Had Pancho's cry been heard? Would someone be running out of the house within the next few seconds?

No one appeared. He glanced at the yellow house next to it. A trim hedgerow bordered the driveway leading to a garage in the rear, and a blue spruce rose elegantly near the center of the small front lawn. It was Roger Hyde's house. In a short while both boys would be coming home from the ball park.

"What're you going to do?" whispered Shadow. "Leave him here? Looks as if he's real hurt."

Skeeter held one hand against the Chihuahua's head, and felt the dog's body with the other. What he hated worse than anything in the world was striking a bird or an animal. Even accidentally. He loved them. He had a white falcon he called Gus — a beautiful, trained bird he had raised from the time it had begun sprouting feathers. Dad had gotten it for him for his ninth birthday. He knew how he'd feel if someone struck Gus and injured him. He'd feel almost as if he, himself, had been injured.

That was probably how Tommy Scott would feel, too. Because Tommy must love Pancho.

Skeeter picked up the little animal and cradled it in his left arm. The Chihuahua lay still, trembling. It licked Skeeter's hand as if it wanted to be friends, as if all that barking had been just to show off.

Skeeter lifted his bike, climbed on it, and started to pedal away.

"Where are you taking him?" Shadow asked as he followed close behind on his bike.

"Home, first. I promised I'd go right home," said Skeeter. "Then to Dr. Wiggins. I think his leg is broken."

The boys rode home. Shadow lived four houses beyond Skeeter's. "I'll meet you in about fifteen minutes and we can go to the vet's," said Skeeter.

Skeeter hid Pancho in a corner of the garage, placing him on an old coat he found in there. He didn't tell anyone about the accident. That had to be just between him and Shadow.

He got out of his uniform, put on regular clothes, and washed. Mom must have noticed that he was very quiet. She always noticed things like that. She asked him if something was wrong and he said no, there's nothing wrong. Why?

"Shouldn't be anything wrong," Bob said. "All he did was single, double, and homer."

That stopped Mom from asking more questions, but she still seemed puzzled about the way he looked. That Mom. She was always more observant about things than Dad was.

Skeeter did a lot of thinking while he changed. Dr. Wiggins, the vet, lived about six blocks away. Suppose someone saw Skeeter taking the Chihuahua there, and this someone recognized the dog? How would Skeeter explain that?

Then he had it figured out. At least, he thought he did. Calling to his mother that he was going for a bike ride with Shadow, he left the house.

He rode over to Shadow's house with two

small baskets, one clinging to each handle-bar. Shadow was waiting for him. He looked at the two baskets and frowned.

"Two baskets?" He looked at Skeeter. "How come two baskets?"

"Just in case," said Skeeter. "Here, you take this one. Be careful. Pancho's in there."

"And what's in that one?" Shadow pointed curiously at the other basket, then started sniffing. "Smells good."

"It is," Skeeter replied, and pedaled ahead of Shadow without telling him what was in the basket.

Tree shadows flickered across their faces as they rode. They passed kids jumping rope and playing catch with a soft ball. Here and there people were sitting on porches, reading the evening paper or just relaxing.

The boys had two blocks to go when a shout sprang from behind them.

"Hey, Skeet! Shadow!"

"Oh-oh!" murmured Shadow.

Skeeter looked over his shoulder. For an instant, panic shot through him. Four guys were coming up behind them on bikes, including Roger Hyde and Tommy Scott!

"What shall we do, Skeet?" Shadow cried softly.

"Act natural," replied Skeeter. "I'll handle it."

Roger was first to reach them. "Where are you guys going with those baskets?" he wanted to know.

Skeeter looked at him and then at the others. He flashed a smile. "Are you guys good guys or bad guys?" he asked jokingly. He glanced at Tommy Scott, saw the sober, rather sad look on Tommy's face. His heart ached again. He wanted to tell Tommy not to worry, that he had Pancho, and that he was taking him to a doctor. But he couldn't tell that to Tommy. Not yet. Not until he knew that Pancho would be all right.

The guys laughed, all except Tommy.

Skeeter turned his attention back to his driving. At the same time he veered his bike slightly to get closer to Roger.

"We're bad guys," said Roger out of the corner of his mouth. "This is a holdup." Then he grinned and sniffed the air. "Hey! Whatever's in that basket smells good!"

"Doughnuts," said Skeeter. "I'm taking them to my aunt and uncle's." He slowed down and braked the bike to a halt. "Wait a minute. There's plenty in our two baskets for an army. You guys want one?"

Roger looked at him in surprise. "I only *said* this was a holdup, Skeet. I didn't *mean* it."

"I know you didn't," replied Skeeter. "Take one, anyway."

He pulled back the white linen cloth that

covered the doughnuts and lifted one out for each of the four boys. They were large, powder-sugared doughnuts and still warm.

"Thanks, Skeet!" Roger's eyes went almost as wide as the doughnut holes. "H'mmm! They smell delicious!"

The other boys paid their thanks to Skeeter, and then turned their bikes and rode off.

"Yokies," said Shadow, wiping his brow with his forefinger. "It's a good thing you figured that out or we'd have been sunk."

Skeeter grinned. "Just leave it to me," he said triumphantly.

He got to thinking about Tommy, and the grin faded. No matter what he had thought of Tommy's ability as a baseball player, deep inside Skeeter felt awful.

He loved animals so much. Why had Pancho taken that moment to run in front of him and be struck by his bike? Why?

4

Dr. Wiggins lived in a white sprawling house with a large green lawn around it. Flowers grew alongside the driveway and up a lattice that stood on either side of the front porch.

There were three people in the waiting room, each patiently holding a dog. Skeeter and Shadow had to wait for half an hour before their turn came.

Dr. Wiggins was a tall man with gray, friendly eyes peering through horn-rimmed glasses. He and Skeeter had become acquainted when Gus, the falcon, had gotten sick. Skeeter had taken it to the vet and in a short time Gus was well again.

After the doctor greeted the boys, he looked curiously at the basket and then at Skeeter. "Gus isn't sick again, is he?" he asked.

"No. This is Pancho, a Mexican Chihuahua," Skeeter explained. "He doesn't belong to me. I hit him accidentally with my bike."

Dr. Wiggins uncovered the trembling little animal, lifted it out of the basket, and laid it gently on a table. He ran his fingers carefully over the tiny body and then paused at a spot on the dog's rear left leg and rubbed his thumb over it. Pancho whimpered and tried to lift his head, but the doctor held it down.

"Bone broken in the leg," Dr. Wiggins observed. "Needs to be set and splinted. That might not be all, though. If the wheel of your bike ran over part of his stomach it could've caused an internal injury. I think you'd better leave Pancho here a few days, Skeeter."

A lump rose in Skeeter's throat. "Is he real bad, Dr. Wiggins?"

The doctor shrugged. "I'm not sure, Skeeter. I won't know for sure until I see how really serious the damage is. Call back in a few days. By then I should know how he is."

Skeeter took the sack of doughnuts out of the basket Shadow was holding and placed it on the table.

"What's that?" asked Dr. Wiggins.

"Doughnuts," replied Skeeter humbly. "You can have them. There's no sense taking them back. If those guys stopped us again and smelled the doughnuts we wouldn't know what to say to them, because I told them we were taking them to my aunt and uncle's."

"What guys?" asked the doctor curiously.

So Skeeter and Shadow told him about meeting Roger and the others and giving them doughnuts and telling them that they were taking the doughnuts to Skeeter's aunt and uncle's. Skeeter said he just didn't feel like riding all the way out in the country to Aunt Phyllis and Uncle Rob's now.

The doctor lifted a doughnut out of the sack between his thumb and forefinger, squeezed it gently, and smiled. "Well! If all the doughnuts are like this one, I'm not going to argue with you!"

The boys rode home. Skeeter parked the bike in the garage and walked with a heavy heart to the back porch. In the large screened-cage in the corner, built level with the windows so that it could look out-of-doors, was the white falcon Gus.

His head jerked erect as Skeeter's footsteps sounded on the porch. A large eye, glued upon Skeeter, was briefly covered as an eyelid went down and up again.

"Hi, Gus," said Skeeter. The falcon answered with a soft cackle.

Skeeter opened the cage, called to the falcon, and the big bird stepped out and climbed upon Skeeter's arm. It was heavy, its white plumage like snow.

"Want to exercise your wings a little?" Skeeter smiled. He walked to the porch door, stretched out his arm, and the falcon took off with a *whoosh!* of its huge, pointed wings. The wings flapped quickly for a while as the big white bird climbed higher and higher, flying over the houses and the towering trees.

Skeeter watched, with a bright glow in his eyes, as his winged friend sailed freely around in the sky. A few minutes later the falcon returned, landing on the wooden perch that extended from the rail of the porch steps Dad had made expressly for this purpose. From there it climbed up on Skeeter's arm and Skeeter returned it to its cage.

At baseball practice the next morning, Skeeter noticed that Tommy Scott seemed even more troubled than he was last evening. The first thing he heard was, "Something's happened to Tommy's dog, that little Mexican Chihuahua. He disappeared yesterday."

He trotted to the outfield and shagged flies which a high school boy was hitting out to them. Another high school boy was working with the infielders.

There was batting practice afterwards, but Skeeter remained in the outfield. He didn't come to bat until one of the guys yelled for him to come in and hit. He didn't want to bat even then. But if he didn't, someone might wonder what was bothering him.

He swung at two pitches and missed completely. Then he hit two grounders, popped one to the pitcher, and missed again.

Roger Hyde, standing in center field with his arms folded, roared out in laughter. "What happened, slugger? I thought you were a fence buster?"

Skeeter telephoned Dr. Wiggins that afternoon. Pancho's condition was still critical, said the doctor. He had placed a splint on the broken leg, but he was not yet able to tell whether the little Chihuahua might survive its internal injuries.

"I have a hunch he'll come through, though, Skeeter," added the doctor. "Don't worry."

He just says that to make me feel better, thought Skeeter.

A few days later he changed into his baseball uniform in preparation for the game against the Dinosaurs and heard his father calling to him. Dad was reading the *Crown Point Journal* in the living room. "There's a notice here in the Lost and Found column about Tommy Scott's pet dog, Pancho," he said. "Says Pancho's lost or stolen. Have you heard about it, Skeeter?"

Skeeter's neck reddened. "Yes. Heard it last week. Tommy told us at practice."

"That's a shame. That was a cute little dog, that Chihuahua."

5

Skeeter wasn't himself as he stood beside the dugout and waited for his turn to bat. He couldn't get Pancho out of his mind.

Tip and Joey both struck out. Roger banged out a single and Skeeter stepped to the plate. There was a girl sitting in the bleachers behind the Milky Ways' dugout and shouting as if she were the only Milky Ways fan there. She had yelled for Tip and Joey and Roger to hit. Now she was yelling for Skeeter.

He took a called strike and two balls.

Then he swung at a belt-high pitch and missed for strike two.

He stepped out of the box, rubbed his sweating hands on the bat, and stepped in again.

The pitch came in, a little high and close to the outside corner. He swung.

"Strike three!" cried the umpire as the bat swished through the air.

A disappointed moan broke from the girl in the stands.

No balls came out to Skeeter during the second half of the inning. In the next inning a high fly was hit to deep left. Skeeter watched it soar into the blue sky and thought for sure that it was heading for the fence behind him. He turned and rushed back, stumbled, regained his footing, turned again.

His eyes widened in horror as he saw the ball coming down far in front of him. Boy,

had he misjudged that one! He bolted forward, running as hard as he could. When he
saw that he would not be able to catch it by
running, he dove at it. The ball brushed the
tip of his glove and struck the ground, and
he went sprawling forward on his stomach.

He scrambled to his feet, picked up the
ball, and pegged it to second. The man was
already there.

Laughter exploded from the Dinosaurs'
fans.

"Holy cow, Skeet!" exclaimed third baseman Henry Mall. "If you'd stayed in your
position you could've caught that ball in
your hip pocket!"

In the third inning he misjudged another
fly. He thought this one was going to land almost in the exact spot where he was standing. He realized it wasn't when it began
sailing over his head. By that time he wasn't
able to get back fast enough. The ball

bounced out to the fence. He raced after it, picked it up, and threw it in. The hitter stopped on third base for a triple.

A single drove in the run, and the Dinosaurs led 3 to 1. Roger caught a high fly in deep center for the third out of the inning and trotted in with a cocky look on his face. Near the dugout the expression changed to one of disgust as he looked at Skeeter. Skeeter pretended he didn't see it.

At the plate, things were a little different. Skeeter had forgotten his worries about Pancho after the first inning. His second time up he slashed out a three-bagger. On his third time up he hit a homer with two on.

"Thataway, Skeeter!" yelled the girl in the stands.

Tommy Scott replaced him in the fifth. He corked a single, then got out when he failed to tag up on a caught fly ball.

The side was retired. Roger, running out

to his position in center field, patted Tommy on the shoulder.

It's okay to be pals, thought Skeeter, *but why does Roger prefer to have Tommy play instead of me? Anybody can see that Tommy is no hitter. And he really isn't much better than I am in the outfield.*

The game ended with the Milky Ways winning 8 to 5.

The next afternoon Skeeter telephoned Dr. Wiggins and received some happy news.

"Yes, Pancho is coming along fine, Skeeter," said the doctor. "You can come over and take him home, but better watch him for a few days. Don't let him run around. And see that he is fed only once each day and very little, at that."

Skeeter got the basket in which he had taken Pancho to the vet, and went over to Shadow's house. He told Shadow that he was going to pick up Pancho and take him to

Aunt Phyllis and Uncle Rob's and asked if Shadow would like to go along.

"Of course," said Shadow. "But I can't go on my bike. I've got a flat."

"Okay. We'll walk," said Skeeter. "It's only a little way out."

So the two of them walked to Dr. Wiggins's office and picked up Pancho. Skeeter was worried about how to pay the doctor. He didn't have much money in his bank. Dr. Wiggins's bill surely would be much more than he had. Well, whatever it was, he'd earn money somehow to pay for it.

Pancho didn't look any different than on the day Skeeter had taken him to the vet. Guess he just couldn't be any skinnier, or fatter. The splint was still on his leg. He'd need it for another week or so, explained the doctor.

Skeeter was embarrassed when the moment came to ask for the bill. Finally he asked, and then waited to hear the doctor mention a large sum. After all, besides fixing up Pancho, the doctor had housed the dog for almost a week.

Dr. Wiggins looked seriously at Skeeter, then at Shadow. "Remember those doughnuts you gave me?" he said, pressing a hard finger against Skeeter's chest. "Bring me another half a dozen sometime and we'll call it square. Fair enough?"

Skeeter stared at him.

"Get out of here." The doctor motioned as if he were in a hurry to get rid of them. "And don't forget those doughnuts. Okay?"

"Yes, sir!" smiled Skeeter, and hustled out of the room with Pancho nestled in the basket and Shadow at his heels.

Four blocks and they were out of the village. They began climbing the hill that led to Aunt Phyllis and Uncle Rob's home.

"Shadow, remember me telling you that

we're going to visit my aunt and uncle in Idaho sometime this summer?" Skeeter said.

"Yes. Said you're going when your dad has his vacation."

"Right. Well, it starts next Monday, so we're leaving this Saturday by jet."

"Boy! Wish I could go with you! I've never ridden on a jet. Have you?"

"No." But flying by jet wasn't what he was thinking about. "Shadow, will you take care of my pet falcon Gus while we're gone?"

"Sure I will."

"Thanks. All you have to do is feed him once in the morning and once at night. A small cup and the feed are next to his cage. Let him out once in a while for exercise. He'll fly back after five minutes or so."

"It'll be a cinch, Skeet," said Shadow.

A car drove up beside them and stopped. "Want a ride?" a voice asked. It was Tommy Scott! And behind the wheel was the girl from the baseball game! The girl who had done all that crazy shouting!

Skeeter blushed. He put his hand, which had suddenly begun to tremble, over the white linen cloth which covered Pancho. "No, thanks," he said nervously. "We're not going far."

"Oh, get in, Skeeter," persuaded the girl, smiling good-naturedly. "We can talk baseball. I'm Jan, Tommy's sister. And you're Shadow, aren't you?" She looked at Shadow.

"Yes," said Shadow, bobbing his head.

"You sure you don't want to ride?" said Tommy. Skeeter realized now how closely the girl resembled him.

"We're sure," he replied, and tried to smile. "We don't mind walking."

Just then the tiny warm animal under Skeeter's hand stirred. Then he barked. And he barked again and again.

6

Skeeter stared at the lumpy linen cloth stirring in the basket and then at Tommy and his sister Jan. He wished he could disappear then and there. Or that the world would swallow him up. Anything so he wouldn't have to face those two in the car.

"That's Pancho!" Tommy cried. "You've got Pancho in that basket!"

The little Mexican Chihuahua struggled free of the cloth and poked his small head out of the basket. His big round eyes saw Tommy and he barked again. A happy bark, followed by a whimper.

Tommy opened the door, jumped out and picked the little animal up into his arms. "Pancho!" he cried, cuddling the chihuahua. "My Pancho!"

"Skeeter!" exclaimed Tommy's sister, her brown eyes growing wide as chestnuts. "*You* took Pancho!"

"I didn't *steal* him," said Skeeter, his throat suddenly aching terribly.

"We were going to bring him back," Shadow explained. "Just as soon as he got well again."

"Well again?" Tommy's hot eyes shot from Skeeter to Shadow. "What do you mean 'well again'?" And then he noticed the splint on Pancho's leg. "What's this?"

"I struck him with my bike," confessed Skeeter, unable to look Tommy directly in the eyes.

"You struck him, and you never told me? You — you nut!"

"Tommy!" yelled his sister. "Let Skeeter explain, will you?"

Skeeter took a deep breath, let it out, then explained how he had accidentally struck Pancho with his bike, and how he had taken the little animal to Dr. Wiggins and had left it there and why he was taking it to Aunt Phyllis and Uncle Bob's now.

"I — I was going to bring Pancho back to you as soon as he got real well again," Skeeter finished, glad that at last he had the secret off his chest.

"You should've told me about it when it happened," Tommy shot back angrily. "I thought somebody had stolen him! Just like Roger says — you're a meathead! A hundred percent meathead!"

He jumped into the car, his eyes wet and blazing.

"Tommy," said his sister, calmly, "Skeeter did what he thought best. He took Pancho

44

to the vet, didn't he? He helped save Pancho's life." She turned to the boys. An apologetic look came over her face. Then a smile. "Get in, boys. I'll take you home."

"No, thanks," said Skeeter. "We can walk back."

The girl looked at him. The smile faded a little. "Well, guess I can't blame you. Thanks very much for what you did for Pancho."

She released the brake, stepped on the accelerator, and drove off. Skeeter and Shadow headed back down the hill for home.

"You can't win," murmured Shadow disgustedly.

"Guess maybe I should've told him so he wouldn't have worried so," said Skeeter. "Guess that's what I should've done, Shadow. You saw his face the minute he saw Pancho. He almost cried he was so happy."

"Yes. I saw him," said Shadow.

The Milky Ways played the Dragonflies on Thursday. Skeeter had planned to tell Coach Jess O'Hara after the game about his going to Idaho, but the coach had already known about it. Some of the guys had told him.

Jimmy Sutton started in left field instead of Skeeter. He caught a couple of flies and popped to short. Skeeter took his place in the third inning and the first time he doubled. It was the second hit off Cal Fielding, the Dragonflies' star right-handed pitcher. Roger Hyde had got the first one.

Bogy Adams corked a line drive to right center which the fielder caught on the first hop. Skeeter tore around third and bolted for home in a desperate attempt to beat the throw.

"Slide, Skeeter!" someone shouted.

"Hit it, Skeet!" yelled the coach. "Hit the dirt!"

He was sure he would make it without sliding, though. He could tell by the look on the catcher's face that the ball wasn't anywhere near home yet.

And then, within two steps of the plate, the catcher caught the relayed throw-in from the pitcher and tagged Skeeter. "Out!" yelled the umpire.

"You meathead!" yelled Roger. "Why didn't you hit the dirt? You would've been safe!"

Skeeter ran to the dugout, his head bowed. He wouldn't admit he was scared to slide.

He socked a long one to deep center the next time up. The fielder just barely caught it. The third time up he singled. But in the outfield he missed three, the third one happening with the score tied and a man on third. It decided the game. The Dragonflies edged out the Milky Ways, 4 to 3.

Jess O'Hara put an arm around Skeeter's shoulder and smiled. "Skeeter, you've got the eyes of a hawk when it come to batting. But in the outfield they don't seem to do much good, do they?"

Skeeter nodded sadly. "Guess not," he admitted.

"Well, you just keep hitting that ball. That's what brings in the runs," said the coach. "And — oh, yes — have a nice time in Idaho."

"Thanks," replied Skeeter.

7

Early Saturday morning Mom, Dad, Bob, and Skeeter took a taxi to the airport, where they boarded a plane to New York City. In New York they got on a jetliner for Idaho. It was the thrill of a lifetime for Skeeter. He had seen jets flying thousands of feet in the air, but never had he been near one. Now had come the greatest moment of all. He was going to ride in one.

Mom and Dad sat together in the big plane and Skeeter sat with Bob, Skeeter next to the window. The jet taxied down the runway, gained speed rapidly, then lifted into the air.

Skeeter felt a strange sensation in his stomach as he watched the earth seeming to fall farther and farther away below them. The ground became a blanket of many colors. The trees, houses, and the moving automobiles began to look like tiny models.

They sped on, rising higher and higher, until they flew through thick blankets of clouds and then above them. Overhead was the ocean of blue sky. Skeeter watched with awe. *What a ride!* he thought.

They had lunch on the plane. They crossed over rivers and lakes, tiny towns and great cities. They stopped once on their route, dispatching passengers and picking up new ones.

Late that afternoon the jetliner landed

at Boise Airport. From there the Miracles took a limousine service to Spring City, fifty miles away. Uncle Don and Aunt Arlene and Skeeter's cousins Alan and Tina Rose were waiting for them.

How big Alan was! thought Skeeter. And the last time he had seen Tina Rose was when she was a baby. That was five years ago.

Uncle Don looked a little like Dad. That was, of course, because they were brothers. Guess by the way they shook hands and smiled at each other they just couldn't wait for this moment to come — when they could go hunting and fishing together again for a while.

As they rode in Uncle Don's station wagon to their home, Skeeter looked at the buildings and streets almost with disappointment. "Spring City's no different from home," he said.

Bob chuckled. "What did you expect to see? Dirt roads for streets and horse and wagons instead of cars?"

Skeeter shrugged. "I don't know. The only big difference seems to be the hilly streets."

"Idaho's full of mountains," said Alan, who was sitting beside him.

"Is there any place flat enough to play baseball?"

Alan laughed. "Oh, sure. We even have a Midget League. I play second base on our team, the Deerslayers."

"Good! How's the team?"

"We're okay. Just unlucky."

Skeeter looked at him. "What do you mean?"

"Well, we're in fifth place. Next to the bottom. We ought to be in second, at least. Do you play, Skeet?"

Skeeter nodded and caught Bob's eyes

smiling at him. Alan saw it, too. He grinned. "I suppose you're the star, or something?" he said.

"You might call it that," said Bob.

"I'm no star," corrected Skeeter. "I've got a dozen feet when I'm chasing a ball in the outfield, and they're all going in different directions. Only thing I can do is hit."

"I'm just fair," admitted Alan. "I can't hit and can't field."

Uncle Don stopped at a red light, and Skeeter noticed how steep the street was. There weren't many people on the sidewalk. Other than being hilly, everything was like back home.

The Skeeter heard a loud, rackety sound to his right. Two boys were whizzing down the sidewalk on skateboards. They were sitting down, their knees drawn up and their hands clutching the narrow sides.

"Wow!" exclaimed Skeeter. "Those guys are really moving!"

"That's because of the hilly streets, I suppose," Alan replied. "We have races here, too. Slaloms, they're called. The streets are blocked off and cans are put every few yards apart, and you skateboard in and out of them. It's fun."

"I bet," said Skeeter. The two boys on the skateboards were turning the corner, their bodies leaning far over to their right side. An instant later they were out of sight around the buildings. Boy! thought Skeeter. Can they ride those things!

"Can you skateboard?" Alan asked.

"No. But I'd sure like to. A lot of kids back home skateboard, but Mom and Dad think it's dangerous."

"They are if you're not careful," admitted Alan. "It takes a lot of practice to be good. After that it's easy."

A thought occurred to Skeeter. "Do you have a skateboard, Alan?"

"Oh, sure. Most kids I know . . ."

There was another loud rackety sound. This time three kids, two of them girls, were riding skateboards down the sidewalk. "That's Jim Buckley," said Alan. "He's an outfielder on our team."

"Those children!" Mom cried. "Aren't they afraid?"

Aunt Arlene laughed and waved a hand, and you knew that this sight wasn't anything new to her.

Aunt Arlene cooked supper. Afterwards Skeeter asked Mom and Dad if he could go out and ride Alan's skateboard.

Mom and Dad exchanged looks, and for a moment Skeeter's hopes began to fade. He knew they were afraid he might get hurt.

"I won't get hurt," he promised, a pleading look in his eyes.

"He'll be all right if he stays on the sidewalk next to the house," said Bob. "He can't get too hurt where it's level."

Mom and Dad looked at each other again. Then Dad nodded, giving his okay. "All right," said Mom. "But be careful."

Skeeter grinned at them. "Thanks!"

"Just remember that you don't want to be on the disabled list if the Milky Ways need your hitting," reminded Dad.

"Who's going to get hurt?" cried Skeeter. "Come on, Alan! Let's go!"

Alan got his skateboard and they went outside. The skateboard was really jazzy looking — bright blue with silver zigzags and neat stickers Alan must have collected. Skeeter couldn't wait to try it out.

"Put your left foot on the board and push yourself along with your other foot," said Alan. "Like this."

He showed Skeeter what he meant. After the skateboard got rolling, Alan placed his other foot on the board too, coasted to the street sidewalk, turned around, and stopped just inside the yard. He gave a hard push with his right foot and the skateboard coasted to the end of the walk where Skeeter stood waiting.

Then Skeeter tried it. He started off exactly as Alan had. But he had hardly traveled ten feet when the skateboard started for the lawn.

"Lean to the right!" shouted Alan.

Skeeter leaned to the right, but the skateboard kept going straight ahead and rolled off the sidewalk. The skateboard slowed down as if it had struck molasses, and Skeeter went running off it to keep from falling.

Bob, who was relaxing on a lawn swing, laughed. "You have to lean with your feet, too," he said. "That's how to steer it. Use your head."

Skeeter laughed, too. "Make up your mind. My feet, or my head?"

He improved with each try, and finally managed to coast all the way to the street sidewalk.

"Look, Alan! I did it!" he cried happily.

Then fear gripped him. He couldn't turn around. He tried to lean over, to steer the skateboard with his feet. It turned a little, but not enough. It was heading for the street. And there was a car coming down.

8

Skeeter's mind worked quickly. He lowered himself on the skateboard so that he was almost sitting on it, clutched its sides, then sprang out both feet and pressed them against the sidewalk. He came to a stop right at the edge of the curb.

He looked up just as the car drove past. The driver didn't give him as much as a glance.

"Boy! That was quick thinking!" said Alan, running up behind him.

Skeeter turned the skateboard around on

the walk. "One thing I have to learn," he observed, "is to steer this thing."

"It's easy once you get used to it," said Alan.

After a while Skeeter realized that he wasn't going to learn to skateboard in one easy lesson. It certainly was going to take more than a couple hours. He got tired of it and asked Alan if he'd like to play catch.

"Sure!" said Alan. He started running into the house, then stopped. "I've only got one glove."

"Can't you get another one?"

"I'll borrow Jim's," said Alan. "Come on over and meet him."

Jim Buckley lived on another block. Skeeter remembered him riding a skateboard like a blue streak down a sidewalk.

Jim pushed back a lock of dark brown hair and stuck out a hand as Alan introduced him to Skeeter. "Okay if the three of us play?" he asked. "I've got two gloves."

"Sure," said Alan. The three boys played until it got dark, which wasn't long afterwards. Then the two families sat in the living room and talked and talked till Skeeter couldn't keep his eyes open another minute. Tina Rose had been put in bed and only the grown-ups seemed able to stay up a lot longer.

Skeeter plopped into bed with Alan. They talked until sleep overtook them practically at the same time.

The next morning Skeeter wrote a letter to Shadow.

Dear Shadow,

How is Gus? I hope that you're not having any trouble feeding him. How are your mother and father?

We took a jetliner from New York City. Boy, was it fun! My cousin Alan has a skateboard and I'm learning to ride it. I can ride it pretty good already, but my trouble is steering it. I almost rode it into the street yesterday.

I hope the Milky Ways trim the pants off the Jets tomorrow. And I hope that Roger Hyde and Tommy Scott both strike out every time. . . . No, I don't either. Guess I shouldn't say that. Mom will probably read this letter and she'll probably cross out what I said about those guys. Also I feel sorry for Tommy about his dog Pancho. I guess I'll never forget that. Is he getting along okay? Pancho, I mean.

Thanks for feeding Gus for me. We're all fine.

Your friend,
Skeeter

Mom read the letter, but she didn't cross out a single word. At one part she smiled, and Skeeter figured it was the part about

Roger and Tommy. Dad couldn't read it. He had gone hunting with Bob and Uncle Don before the younger boys had gotten out of bed. Bob had gone along just in hopes he might see a moose, or a mountain lion, or anything else that was big and wild. He carried no gun. He didn't care about hunting.

How was Pancho? Skeeter wondered. Was he able to walk around yet? To run? Then Skeeter realized that it was only a few days ago that he and Shadow had been walking up the road with Pancho inside a basket and Tommy Scott and his sister had come along. What a moment that was! It would be one he'd long remember.

Poor Pancho. And poor Tommy, too. Guess it must've been terrible worrying about Pancho all that time. Not knowing where he was, or what had happened to him. *It was all wrong not to have told*

Tommy about striking the Chihuahua with my bike, thought Skeeter. *I should've told him right away instead of taking Pancho to the vet and then waiting and waiting. No wonder Tommy called me a meathead. I deserved it. His heart must've been busted to pieces all that time.*

Thinking about Pancho made him also think about Gus. He sure missed Gus. Imagine being away from him for almost two weeks. Skeeter had an idea how Tommy must have felt. Only Tommy hadn't known where his pet was, while Skeeter did.

9

Dad, Bob, and Uncle Don came home at five o'clock — empty-handed. Neither Dad nor Uncle Don had fired a shot. But they had seen a moose and a bear, so their trip hadn't been all in vain.

After supper both families went to the baseball part to watch the Deerslayers play the Badgers. The game started at six-thirty. The Deerslayers had last raps. They looked sharp in their white uniforms and blue caps, and Skeeter wished he was out there with them. The first baseman, a tall left-hander, threw a ball around to the infielders, while a small left-handed pitcher threw in warm-up pitches.

Alan wasn't playing. Probably he'd get in later, thought Skeeter.

The infield ball was thrown in toward the Deerslayers' dugout. The umpire yelled, "Play ball!" and the game started. The Deerslayers' infield began a loud, steady chatter.

"Come on, Chuck! Whiff 'im, boy!"

"Breeze it past 'im, Chuck!"

"Easy meat, Chucky, ol' boy!"

Skeeter felt goose pimples pop out on his arms. Everything was the same as back home. The chatter. The talk to the pitcher. The enthusiastic fans.

The little left-hander got a signal from the catcher. He nodded, wound up, delivered. "Strike!" cried the umpire.

Uncle Don tapped Skeeter on the knee. "That's Chuck Kelly pitching," he said. "What do you think of his speed?"

"He's got a lot of it," admitted Skeeter.

Chuck Kelly got two strikes on the batter, then delivered one outside for ball one. The next was low. The batter swung, topped the ball, and it went dribbling toward the pitcher. Chuck fielded it easily and threw the man out.

Chuck struck out the second batter and the third hitter popped to short. The Deerslayers got up and scored a run. Neither team threatened again until the third inning when a Badgers hitter laid into one for a clean triple. The next hitter singled him in, and the next man walked. The Deerslayers coach called time, went out to the mound and talked to Chuck.

"Those two hits shook Chuck up a little." Uncle Don smiled. "Guess that's natural, isn't it?"

"Our pitchers get shook up, too," said Skeeter.

"So do the opposing pitchers after Skeeter tags on to one," put in Bob. "You don't know it, Uncle Don, but that boy sitting beside you leads the Grasshopper League in hits *and* home runs."

"Is that so?" Uncle Don beamed at Skeeter. "Maybe the Deerslayers might like to purchase you for next year, Skeeter — if the price isn't too high, that is," he added, chuckling.

Skeeter grinned. "I'm not for sale," he said. "Anyway, I'm a poor outfielder. I'm all legs when I'm chasing after a fly ball."

"You'll outgrow that," said Uncle Don. "Alan's just the opposite. He can field but he can't hit."

The top half of the third inning ended with the Badgers leading 2 to 1. The Deerslayers came to bat but went down one, two, three.

Alan replaced the Deerslayers' second

baseman in the top of the fourth. A ball came to him, a hot grounder on his left side. He fielded it neatly and threw the man out. A hard-hit ball zipped through the third baseman's legs, putting a man on for the Badgers. The man was put out trying to steal second, and Chuck Kelly struck out the third.

The Deerslayers' lead-off man grounded out in the bottom of the fourth, and Alan was up. He took a count of two and two, then hit a hard grounder through the hole betwcen third and short. The Deerslayers' fans shouted wildly, including Skeeter, Bob, Uncle Don, and the rest of the two families. Alan rounded first and headed for second.

"What's he doing?" cried Uncle Don, rising to his feet. "No! No, Alan!" he shouted.

But Alan kept going. Skeeter's heart pounded as he saw the left fielder pick up the ball and peg it to second.

"Hit the dirt, Alan!" he yelled, his voice drowned out among the cries of the other fans. "Hit it!"

Alan hit the dirt as if he'd heard Skeeter. But the shortstop had caught the ball and tagged Alan a yard in front of the bag. An easy out.

Alan got up and brushed the dust off his pants as he ran across the diamond toward the dugout.

A kid sitting behind the backstop screen stood up and yelled, "What're you trying to do, Alan? Show off for your cousin?"

"Trying to stretch a single into a double, Alan?" yelled another.

Skeeter looked at Uncle Don and smiled. "Everything's like it is back home," he said. "Even the fans."

"Oh, sure," said Uncle Don. "Baseball's the same all over. So are fans."

The Deerslayers' next hitter tripled, and

was knocked in for their second run to tie the score. In the top of the fifth the Badgers got men on first and second. Then Alan caught a hot grounder near the keystone sack, touched the bag, and threw to first for a beautiful double play. The crowd yelled and applauded. The next Badger popped out.

"Here's your chance to win the ball game, Alan!" a fan shouted when Alan came to bat. There was one out and men on first and second.

Alan hit a slow grounder to short. The shortstop played it to second in an effort to get a double play. The runner was out at second, but Alan made it to first in time.

Two outs, runners on first and third. Chuck Kelly was up. He singled to right! A run scored! Alan was held up at third. Good thing he didn't run in then, thought Skeeter. He would've been out again, and then the fans would *really* scream. Well, you had to listen to the first- and third-base coaches. They weren't there for scenery.

The next Deerslayers hitter hit the first pitch to left field and it was caught. They ran out to the field, full of confidence that this game would be theirs. But the Badgers scored twice. The Deerslayers could do nothing during their turn at bat, and the game went to the Badgers, 4 to 3.

Alan and Skeeter walked home together. Alan had his head bowed, unhappy about the whole thing.

"I see what you mean," observed Skeeter. "You guys are unlucky."

"I was thinking about that stupid run I made to second," said Alan.

"Who's perfect?" said Skeeter. "At least you don't get your legs tangled up like I do. And you can field. That double play you made was a honey."

Alan seemed not to have heard him. "You know that hit I got was my first this year?" he said.

Skeeter stared. "It was?"

"That's why I tried to stretch it into a double, I guess."

Skeeter grinned. "We're a couple of mixed-up ball players," he said. "You're a good infielder but a lousy hitter, and I'm a good hitter but a lousy fielder."

He laughed, then Alan laughed. Imagine cousins being mixed-up ball players!

10

Uncle Don and Dad went hunting every day that week and Bob went with them. On Thursday they brought home a moose which Uncle Don said Dad had shot and Dad said Uncle Don had shot. Skeeter figured they both had shot it together. By the expression on their faces, they seemed pretty proud of it, too.

Uncle Don took it to a place to be skinned and taken care of. He offered Dad the antlers if he wanted them, and Dad said he did. He'd have them mounted on a board and hung in his den.

By Friday Skeeter had improved a lot on the skateboard. He had no more trouble skateboarding out to the street sidewalk and making a complete turn. Maybe now Mom and Dad would let him ride it down the sidewalk. He asked them and, after considering it a while, they agreed that it was all right.

"Just be extra careful," Mom warned. "Don't run anyone down."

"Gee, Mom, you don't think I'd try running anyone down, do you?" he said.

"Maybe we ought to buy him one," suggested Dad. "It's no fun for Alan to stand by while Skeeter rides his skateboard."

"Right!" Skeeter's eyes brightened. "I think that's a *good* idea, Dad!"

So Dad and the boys went to a sporting goods store and bought Skeeter a skateboard. The store was where Alan had purchased his, so the two were identical.

"Now we'll have fun together," said Skeeter to his cousin.

There was practically no danger of striking any pedestrian on the sidewalks. Very few people were on them. Jim Buckley came over with his skateboard and the three skateboarded together.

On Friday evening the Deerslayers played another ball game. Skeeter wished that Alan would get a hit or two, but Alan didn't. He did get a walk, though, and scored a run. And the Deerslayers came out on top.

That night Skeeter wrote his second letter to Shadow.

Dear Shadow,

Boy! a week has already gone by. Am I having fun. I've learned to skateboard, and Dad bought one for me. I've been playing with my cousin's.

How's my pet falcon Gus? You've been feeding him regularly, I hope. I know you

have, Shadow. You're a pal. I sure miss
him. I miss you, too. And the other guys.
How are the Milky Ways doing? Uncle
Don and Dad shot a moose. Well, see you
soon. Good-bye.

Your friend,
Skeeter

P.S. My cousin Alan plays second base
with the Deerslayers. They're pretty good.
P.S. Has Tommy Scott been playing regu-
larly?

He mailed the letter the next morning.

They spent that weekend and Monday driving around the countryside. Alan played baseball Monday afternoon and Skeeter rode his skateboard as much as he could. He also played catch with Alan and Jim Buckley. On Tuesday morning, two days before the Miracles were to return home, the Deerslayers permitted Skeeter to have batting practice with them. Jim Buckley handled the team since he was captain and Mr. Thompson, the coach, had to work.

Skeeter faced a tall right-hander and hit the first two pitches directly down the third-base line. "Look," he heard one of the kids say. "He's batting cross-handed!"

Then Skeeter laid into a pitch and sent it sailing over the left-field fence. The next pitch rocketed even further.

"Hey, look!" the same kid exclaimed. "And cross-handed, too!"

Skeeter tossed the bat aside and ran out to shag flies in the outfield. He used Jim Buckley's extra glove.

"Hey, you really hit that apple!" cried Alan.

"Just lucky," said Skeeter.

The time came at last for the Miracles to go home. The moose antlers would be shipped as soon as they were ready, Dad was promised. Skeeter thought he had never had as much fun as he had visiting his cousin Alan. But he was glad that the time had come to go home, too. He missed Gus terribly. He missed Shadow, and the Milky Ways.

Once in a while he had thought about Roger Hyde and Tommy Scott and Pancho. He sure hoped that Pancho was all right again. But he thought mostly about Tommy Scott. Had he played a lot during Skeeter's absence? Had he played well? Real well? Was he as good as Roger seemed to think he was? And then the question that worried Skeeter the most: Had Tommy proven himself to be so good that he'd replace Skeeter as a starter?

The families said their good-byes at the bus station Thursday noon, and the Miracles were on their way home. They boarded a jetliner in Boise, and that evening they were in New York City. From there they boarded a twin-engined plane, arrived at Crown Point at ten o'clock, and took a cab home.

"I've got to see Gus!" Skeeter cried as the cab stopped in front of their house.

He ran along the side of the house to the front porch. He tripped climbing the steps so fast, caught his balance, went on. He got to Gus's cage.

"Gus!" he cried happily. "Gus! I'm back! Come on out! Where are you, you ol' buddy?"

It was moonlight. Gus would have no trouble stepping out of the cage. But Gus didn't step out. Maybe, thought Skeeter, Gus was so surprised to hear his voice he couldn't move.

Skeeter opened the door of the cage and stuck his head inside. "Gus . . ." he started to say, then stared.

The cage was empty.

11

Skeeter wanted to telephone Shadow and ask about Gus, but Mom told him to go to bed, that he could see Shadow tomorrow. He went to bed, but he couldn't sleep. All he thought about was Gus, his pet falcon. Where was Gus? Why wasn't he in his cage? Hadn't Shadow been taking care of him as he'd promised he would?

Eventually he fell asleep. When he awoke he felt the sun's warm rays on the covers. He got up, dressed, and ate. Then he telephoned Shadow.

"Sure, I fed Gus," said Shadow. "At least until he flew away and never came back."

"When — when was that, Shadow?"

"Last Tuesday. I let him out awhile to get some exercise like you had asked me to do. He flew away and never came back. I — I'm awful sorry, Skeeter. I was going to write, but Mom said I might as well wait till you got home."

Skeeter's heart felt like a ball of lead. "I never dreamed he'd fly away and not come back. Okay, Shadow. Thanks very much for feeding him. I'll see you later."

He started to hang up. But Shadow asked him about the trip, so Skeeter told him. After Skeeter hung up he told the bad news about Gus to Mom, Dad, and Bob. It surprised and bothered them almost as much as it had Skeeter.

"Gus might've gotten homesick for you, Skeeter, and gone out looking for you," Dad said. "I've heard of animals doing that. It's possible that some birds would do that, too."

"Especially an intelligent bird like a falcon," Mom added, an encouraging smile in her voice.

Skeeter's hopes went up a few notches. "You mean it's possible that he might fly back home to me?"

Dad nodded. "It's possible."

At ten-thirty Shadow came over with his mother and father. Skeeter and Shadow realized that they couldn't carry on a conversation very well with the grown-ups around, so they retreated to Skeeter's bedroom. Shadow and his parents stayed till noon, then left.

That afternoon some of the guys on the Milky Ways baseball team came to the house: Tip Miles, Joey Spry, Spider, and Leo Sweetman.

"Are we glad to see you!" said Spider.

"How have the Milky Ways been doing?"

asked Skeeter. Practically all of his conversation that morning with Shadow had been about his visit in Idaho.

"Lousy!" answered Tip. "We played three games since you've been gone and lost all three."

"Isn't Tommy Scott doing anything?" Skeeter asked.

"He's doing nothing," Leo Sweetman said disgustedly. "Except striking out or popping up, if you want to call that something. All he got was one hit since you were gone, Skeet. He's no ball player. We need you. We need your hitting *bad.*"

Skeeter turned almost numb. That was the best news he'd heard since coming back from his vacation. At last it must have proven to Roger Hyde that Tommy Scott wasn't a ball player. Not a real good ball player.

Maybe now Roger will change his mind

about me, Skeeter thought. *Sure I miss a fly in the outfield now and then. Sure I'm not the most graceful baseball player on the team. But, at least, I can hit. Everybody admits that.*

Then Skeeter thought of Tommy's pet dog, Pancho — and of his own falcon, Gus. Suddenly he was sorry for Tommy, and didn't care if Tommy started every game during the balance of the baseball season. He knew now how Tommy must've felt when Pancho had turned up missing. Tommy must've felt just as miserable as Skeeter did now.

"You're going to play with us today, aren't you, Skeet?" Joey asked. "We're playing the Dragonflies. They'll swamp us if you don't."

"We need your power, Skeet," said Spider. "Maybe you're no great outfielder, but nobody can beat you at the plate."

Skeeter smiled. Boy, it was good to be

back among the guys again. It seemed as if he'd been gone a whole year instead of only a week and a half.

"Maybe you guys haven't heard that my pet falcon Gus flew away," he said.

"Yes, we did," replied Spider. "Shadow told us. He feels real bad about it. He blames himself."

"It wasn't his fault. I told him to let Gus fly off once in a while for exercise. Gus flew off, and didn't come back."

"Maybe he will sometime," said Joey.

Skeeter shrugged. "I don't know." He took a deep breath, and let it out. "I'll be at the game tonight. But maybe Coach O'Hara won't let me start. Maybe he'll start Tommy Scott. Anyway, that would be all right with me."

The boys stared at him. "Why do you say that?" asked Tip.

"I bet I know," said Spider. "It's because of Pancho, Tommy's dog."

Skeeter remained quiet awhile, then rose from the step and went to the door. "See you guys at the game," he said. He didn't want to talk about Pancho, nor Gus. It was hard enough just thinking about them.

12

Bob had a date that afternoon. Skeeter knew he did because he was whistling one song after another. Girls were pretty funny creatures, Skeeter thought. You'd never catch him whistling just because of some girl.

He went skateboard riding over to Shadow's house. Shadow had never been on a skateboard. He tried to ride Skeeter's, lost his balance the first couple of times and almost fell. But Shadow had good balance. He tried again and stayed on. Skeeter felt certain that Shadow would learn to skateboard much sooner than he had.

"You know what?" Shadow said excitedly. "I'm going to ask Dad to get me one."

"They're fun," said Skeeter. "But you can't be wise with 'em. You've got to be careful."

"Listen to who's giving old Shadow Mc-Fitters advice about being careful!" said Shadow, laughing.

That evening Skeeter went to the ball game and said "Hi" to both Roger Hyde and Tommy Scott. They returned his greeting. Then he asked Tommy how Pancho was.

"He's okay," said Tommy. "He's running and barking as if he'd never been hurt."

"Glad to hear it," said Skeeter.

"I heard your falcon flew away," said Tommy.

Skeeter nodded. "Yeah. Last Tuesday." It choked him to think about Gus.

Coach O'Hara and the other members of the Milky Ways whom Skeeter hadn't seen since his return from vacation welcomed him back warmly. Then he played catch with Luther Lee. Later he heard the coach read off the starting lineup. His name wasn't called.

The Milky Ways had first raps. Skeeter sat in the middle of the dugout, his arms crossed and his legs propped against the supporting post of the dugout. Here he was, he thought, a hitter with a batting average of over .700, warming the bench. It didn't seem sensible. Sure he had felt sorry for Tommy because of what had happened to Pancho. But this was different, wasn't it? This was a crucial baseball game, wasn't it? And didn't the guys say they really needed Skeeter?

On the mound for the Dragonflies was Cal Fielding, who seemed to be extremely nervous today. He was tugging at the visor of his cap, touching his chin and wiggling his shoulders. The Dragonflies began a steady chatter.

Lead-off man Tip Miles dug his rubber cleats into the dirt and waited for Cal to throw. The first two pitches were balls. The third was a strike. Tip lifted his bat higher, moved it back and forth as he waited for the next pitch. He swung. *Crack!* A high fly to short center. The Dragonflies' center fielder came in and took it for the first out.

Joey Spry grounded out to second, bringing up Roger. Cal pulled at his cap, rubbed his chin, and hitched his pants. He threw three consecutive balls, then got one across. The next was low and inside, and Roger walked. That was as far as he got. Bogy struck out on three pitches.

The Dragonflies threatened to score after their lead-off man singled to left and reached second on Tommy Scott's throw-in. Instead of throwing to second, Tommy had thrown to third, so the alert runner had advanced to second.

Skeeter shook his head. Even he knew that the play should've been to second base.

Nick Strope, the Milky Ways' dark-haired right-hander, struck out the next hitter. Third-baseman Henry Mall caught a high-bouncing ball and threw the third hitter out. Then Leo Sweetman caught a pop fly behind home plate to end the threat.

The second inning went by scoreless for both teams, too. The third started off hot for the Milky Ways. Nick Strope singled. Tip Miles walked. Joey Spry got up with the fans really rooting for him. He watched the pitches carefully, got a two-two call, then a three-two.

You could see Joey was really nervous then. He stepped out of the box, rubbed his hands in the dirt, rubbed the dirt off, yanked on his protective helmet, and stepped back in the box. Cal made his stretch, delivered, and Joey swung.

"Strike three!" yelled the umpire. Joey retreated to the dugout, looking like a pup that had lost its bone.

Roger hit an outside pitch past the pitcher that looked good for a hit. Both Nick and Tip started running as hard as they could. The Dragonflies' second baseman raced after the grounder bouncing across the grass near the keystone sack. He made a spectacular back-handed catch of the ball, then stumbled! Quickly he raised to his knees and flipped the ball to the shortstop, who was covering the base.

Out! The shortstop then snapped the ball to first, but too late. Roger was there. Nevertheless, the fans gave the Dragonflies' second baseman a big hand. It was a wonderful play.

Bogy Adams walked, filling the bases.

"Spider! Hold it!"

Spider Webb, on his way to the batting box, halted in his tracks. Coach O'Hara waved him to the bench.

"Okay, Skeeter," the coach said. "Pick up a bat. Get up there and do your stuff."

Skeeter stared. Had he heard right? Or was he dreaming?

"Let's break this game wide open, Skeet," the coach said.

With a nervous look about him, Skeeter climbed out of the dugout. He put on a protective helmet, selected his favorite bat, and went to the batting box.

"Yeah, Skeeter!" the Milky Way fans shouted. "Come on, Skeet! A grand slammer, boy!"

He stepped into the box, faced Cal Fielding, and for the first time in many moons he felt shaky. He had hoped to be in the lineup. He had hoped he could bat when men were on. Now that his hopes were fulfilled, he was scared.

The pitch came in. Skeeter watched it cross the outside corner for a called strike.

The next pitch was across his knees for strike two.

"Step out a second, Skeeter!" advised Coach O'Hara. "Keep loose up there, buddy!"

Skeeter stepped out of the box, jiggled his helmet, wiped sweat from his forehead, stepped back in again.

The pitch breezed in like a bullet. It looked slightly high, but it might be called a strike. It just might.

Skeeter swung.

"You're out!" said the umpire.

13

Skeeter walked back to the dugout, his head bowed, his lips pressed into a thin, straight line. From the third-base side of the bleachers the Dragonflies' fans were yelling and cheering like crazy. With the bases loaded, their pitcher had struck out the league's leading hitter.

Skeeter gathered up his glove from the dugout and started for right field. What a flop he was. Striking out first time up!

"Just a minute, Skeeter," said Coach O'Hara.

Skeeter paused. Now, what? Was the

coach going to yank him from the game
without even giving him a chance in the outfield?

"You all right, Skeet?" the coach asked,
putting a hand on Skeeter's shoulder.

Skeeter nodded. "Yes. I'm okay. Just a little nervous, I guess."

The coach smiled. "That's all I want to
know, Skeeter. Okay, get out there. And
don't miss any fly balls. Okay?"

Skeeter tried not to miss any, but all the
trying in the world didn't help him. He
missed a high fly that struck the fingertips of
his glove and rolled to the fence. The runner
took second on the error. Skeeter's throw-in
to third held him there.

Nick struck the next man out, then caught
a hot liner that was hit in a straight line back
at him. Quickly he spun and threw to second, doubling off the runner before he
could tag up.

Whew! thought Skeeter as he trotted in from the outfield. *That sure saved my life!*

Henry led off and flied out to left field. Leo doubled, but couldn't get past second base. Luther Lee batted for Tommy Scott and struck out, then Nick flied out to end the half inning.

Skeeter chalked up another error when a ball rolled through his legs. Then, with two Dragonflies on base and two outs, he ran in on a high fly, caught it, fumbled it, and caught it again before it could hit the ground. He ran in, holding the ball as tightly as he could.

"For crying out loud, Skeeter!" a fan shouted. "What do you want us to do — have heart failure?"

Skeeter grinned and put a hand over his own pounding heart. Man! He almost had heart failure himself!

Then Skeeter's eyes practically bugged. Jan Scott was sitting with Bob in the stands. So *she* was Bob's girlfriend! How do you like that?

Tip Miles singled to start off the top of the fifth. But again the Dragonflies played well behind their tall right-hander and kept the Milky Ways from scoring.

"Nothing and nothing," muttered Bogy, shaking his head. "We could be here till the sun sets."

"I'll end it the next inning," Skeeter said kiddingly.

Nick lost control of his first pitch to the lead-off hitter and hit him on the thigh. He looked more hurt over it than did the batter, who trotted down to first base, stepped on it, and then began clapping his hands for the next Dragonfly to rap one out of the lot. No Dragonfly rapped one anywhere. Nick struck out the next man. The next grounded out to Joey Spry, and the third popped up to Bogy.

The top of the sixth and Skeeter was up. The scoreboard was a double row of goose eggs. As Skeeter stepped into the box the Milky Way fans began yelling thunderously.

"Rap it, Skeeter! Make up for last time!"

And Jan Scott's voice: "Blast it out of the park, Skeeter!"

He twitched nervously, and wished the people would stop yelling.

"Strike!" cried the umpire. The pitch cut the outside corner.

Skeeter stepped out of the box, rubbed his left hand up and down on the bat, took a deep, hurried breath and stepped in again, holding the bat in his cross-handed way.

The pitch. It was coming across his knees. He couldn't let this one go by. He swung.

A dribbling hit just in front of the plate! He dropped the bat and beat it for first! What a crummy hit! What a real crummy hit!

And then he saw the Dragonflies' first baseman leap. Saw the ball sail over his head to the outfield. "Go! Go! Go!" yelled Joey Spry, coaching at first.

Skeeter touched first and raced to second. The right fielder heaved the ball to second base. A wide throw! The ball bounced out to short left field. Skeeter bolted for third. His helmet fell off, banged on the ground behind him. He ran as if a bear were on his heels.

He reached third. Luther Lee, coaching there, slowed him down — and then waved him home! Skeeter stared for a moment, wondering what had happened. Then he saw the ball, thrown in from short left, strike the ground in front of the third baseman and bounce high over his shoulder toward the bleachers. Skeeter beelined for home.

The Dragonflies' catcher was straddling the plate as if he owned it. Fear overcame Skeeter for one brief moment. Was the play going to be close? Should he slide? Or was the catcher merely trying to fool him?

And then the catcher moved nimbly aside, and Skeeter crossed the plate standing up.

"Thataboy, Skeeter!" Jan Scott's scream practically drowned out all the others'. "A home run!"

Laughter and applause exploded from the Milky Way fans. A home run on a crazy dribbling hit! Of course, it was no home run. It wasn't even a single. There had been errors all around.

Skeeter shook his head unbelievingly as he trotted to the dugout and sat down. The guys pounded him on the knees and shoulders. "Thataway to run, Skeet! You had those guys throwing the ball all over the lot!"

That was the only score the Milky Ways chalked up that inning. But it was enough. The Dragonflies failed to score during their turn at bat and the tense, nerve-tingling game went to the Milky Ways.

14

On Tuesday, August 8, the Milky Ways played the Barracudas. Tony Chavez, pitching for the Barracudas, had the Milky Ways eating out of his hand. All, that is, except Skeeter Miracle, who was hitting the ball as if he knew nothing else. The first time up he connected with an over-the-fence homer. The second time up a triple. The third time up he flied out to deep center.

"You're back in the groove!" yelled his most enthusiastic rooter, Jan Scott, who was sitting, as usual, in the bleachers beside

Bob. On either side of them were their parents, the Scotts and the Miracles.

The Milky Ways won 4 to 2.

As Skeeter started walking off the field with Mom, Dad, and the others, a voice piped up beside him. "Nice game, Skeeter."

He turned, and was almost floored. It was Tommy Scott!

"Thanks, Tommy," he said. Right behind Tommy was Roger Hyde. He didn't expect a word from Roger. But Roger said, "Nice game, Skeeter," and he was almost floored again.

"Thanks, Roger," he answered. He just couldn't get over it. Imagine *them* being nice to him!

The Milky Ways played their last game of the season on Thursday against the Jets who, so far, had nine wins and two losses to lead the league.

There was a change in the lineup. Bogy had gotten into a hitting slump two weeks ago and was still in it, so Coach O'Hara shifted Bogy to eighth position in the batting order. The lineup:

T. Miles	ss
J. Spry	2b
R. Hyde	cf
S. Miracle	rf
H. Mall	3b
L. Sweetman	c
L. Lee	lf
B. Adams	1b
S. McFitters	p

The Jets had first raps. Their lead-off man blasted a hot liner directly at Shadow. It was so hard that it glanced off Shadow's glove and bounced out toward second base. Joey fielded it but held up on throwing when he saw that he couldn't get the runner.

The infielders played in close then, expecting a bunt. It was a bunt, down the third-base line. Henry fielded it, pegged to first for the out. A pop-up and a grounder to short spoiled the Jets' chances of scoring.

The Milky Ways started off with Tip Miles striking out and Joey grounding out. Roger blistered a hard grounder to short which looked like a sure out. But the ball rolled through the shortstop's legs and Roger was on.

Skeeter took a called strike, then two balls. The fourth was in there letter-high. He swung and smashed it out to left center for two bases. Roger held up at third. Henry Mall singled, scoring Roger and Skeeter. Then Leo flied out.

The Jets picked up a run in the second

and another in the third. In the bottom of the third Joey Spry surprised everyone with a clout that was the farthest he had hit since he had started playing baseball. It just cleared the center-field fence for a home run. Roger flied out, then Skeeter came through with his second hit, a triple against the left-field fence. Henry squeezed him in, gaining first base himself on an error by the third baseman.

With the score 4 to 2 in the Milky Ways' favor, the Jets came back strong in the top of the fourth, sending three runs across the plate. Two of them were due to a fly ball which everybody else would have caught — but not Skeeter Miracle. The ball was on a line to short right. Skeeter, thinking he could make a shoestring catch, dove for it, missed it, then scrambled to his feet and raced after the ball, which had rolled out to the fence.

Nothing more happened until the sixth when the Jets increased their margin to six runs against the Milky Ways' four. The Milky Ways were downcast. This was the final game, a game they had hoped very much to carry home in their pockets. Skeeter, especially, had hoped they would win it. After all, the Jets had already won nine, the Milky Ways only six. And Skeeter hadn't played against the Jets since before his trip to Idaho.

But things looked too dark now. It was almost hopeless to expect to overcome the Jets' two-run lead.

Shadow McFitters led off. One, two, three — he went down swinging. Tip Miles fouled off two pitches, took a ball, then flied out to center.

The fans on the third-base side of the bleachers were quieter than Skeeter had ever heard them. There was not even a peep from Jan Scott, who usually yelled something even when the Milky Ways trailed. They just seemed to be waiting for the game to die.

Then the Milky Ways got a break. Jimmy Sutton, who had gone into the game for Joey Spry in the fourth inning, drew a walk, bringing up Roger Hyde. Roger looked the pitches over carefully, then rapped out a double to right center field! Jimmy advanced to third.

All at once the Milky Way fans came to life. "Keep it going, Skeeter! Keep it alive!"

Skeeter stepped to the plate with confidence. Dick Cannon, the southpaw on the mound for the Jets, looked at Skeeter, got his signal, stretched, threw.

Skeeter rapped it. A hard grounder in the hole between third and short! Jimmy Sutton scored! Roger scored! The game was tied up! Skeeter went to second on the throw-in to home.

The Milky Way fans screamed their heads off. The fans who had started to leave sat down again. This game wasn't over yet!

I've got to get in somehow, thought Skeeter. *Come on, Henry. Hit it!*

Two balls, one strike.

Three balls. And then —

"Ball four!" shouted the umpire and pointed at first base.

The Milky Way fans kept yelling. On second base Skeeter crouched with his hands on his knees, ready to go on a hit.

The pitch. Leo swung. *Crack!* A hard grounder through short! Skeeter beelined for third, saw the third-base coach winding his arms like a windmill, urging him to keep going. Skeeter stepped on third, raced for home. He ran as he had never run before.

His helmet blew off and was thumping on the basepath behind him.

He saw the catcher crouched at the plate waiting for the throw-in. From the catcher's expression, from the way he was reaching forward, Skeeter knew that the ball was coming in. He knew that it was a race between him and the ball.

For a second he thought about sliding, and fear clutched him. But it was the thing to do if he were to be safe.

He went down, pushing dirt ahead of him with his heels. He slid across the plate between the catcher's outspread legs.

"Safe!" yelled the umpire.

The stands echoed and reechoed with cheers and shouts as Skeeter scrambled to his feet amid the cloud of dust and trotted happily to the dugout. The whole team came out and swarmed around him.

The ball game was over. The Milky Ways had won.

I did it! Skeeter said proudly to himself. *I slid! And it's easy! It's much easier than I had thought!*

After the shouting died, after Jan and Bob and everybody else congratulated him, he felt a tug at his elbow. It was Tommy Scott and Roger Hyde. Both were smiling.

"Nice game, Skeeter," said Tommy. "Maybe you're no fly catcher, but you can sure wallop that apple."

"Skeeter," Roger said, his face a little red as if he were sort of nervous about something. "I'm sorry about the way I've been acting toward you."

"Forget it," said Skeeter. "I know I'm a clown out there, but I just can't help it. I'm just clumsy, that's all there is to it."

Roger grinned. "Well, I want to tell you

something about Tommy. He's a good friend of mine, so I wanted to do something for him. He loves baseball more than anything. Except for his dog Pancho maybe!" He laughed. "But he talks and dreams about baseball. I had hoped that Coach O'Hara would let him play more than a couple of innings a game. But he didn't. Then while you were in Idaho, he was given a chance to play more."

"And all I did was help the *other* teams win," put in Tommy. "Guess I'll be a sports announcer when I grow up. That's the next best thing."

Roger and Skeeter laughed. "There's another reason, too, Skeet. You played like a clown in the outfield, but you hit that ball better than anyone else in the league. Guess I just didn't think that was fair."

"Who did?" said Skeeter, his eyes shining

happily. "Who cares anymore now, anyway? The season's over and we didn't do so badly as a team, did we? And I'm sure glad Pancho is okay, Tommy. I really am."

"Thanks, Skeeter. And I hope Gus comes back. I know how you must feel."

Skeeter grinned, but for a second he blinked a little.

"Come on, you guys!" he cried. "Let's catch up with Shadow!"

The four boys started off the field together. They walked out of the park and down the street where Skeeter lived, carrying on a constant chatter about the game.

Presently Shadow stopped and stared at the sky. "Skeeter," he whispered. "Look!"

Skeeter stopped and looked. His skin prickled. Flying across the sky was a bird with large, outspread wings that rose and fell slowly and tiredly, as if it had been on a long, long journey somewhere. Then it started downward, the sun striking its snow-white wings as it headed for one of the houses on the street.

"It's Gus!" Skeeter shouted. "It's Gus! He's come home!"

Matt Christopher®

Lance Armstrong

Kobe Bryant

Terrell Davis

Julie Foudy

Jeff Gordon

Wayne Gretzky

Ken Griffey Jr.

Mia Hamm

Tony Hawk

Grant Hill

Ichiro

Derek Jeter

Randy Johnson

Michael Jordan

Mario Lemieux

Tara Lipinski

Mark McGwire

Greg Maddux

Hakeem Olajuwon

Shaquille O'Neal

Alex Rodriguez

Briana Scurry

Sammy Sosa

Venus and
Serena Williams

Tiger Woods

Steve Young

The #1 Sports Series for Kids

MATT CHRISTOPHER®

Read them all!

*Previously published as *Crackerjack Halfback*

All available in paperback from Little, Brown and Company